To Mackenzie and CJ —WB   To Sheila, wedding consultant extraordinaire! —KH

Number pending. ISBN 978-1-5362-0884-9. This book was typeset in ITC Espirit. The illustrations were done in acrylic and ink.
Candlewick Press, 99 Dover Street, Somerville, Massachusetts 02144. www.candlewick.com.
Printed in Humen, Dongguan, China. 21 22 23 24 25 26 APS 10 9 8 7 6 5 4 3 2 1

THERE'S A
DODO
~ ON THE ~
WEDDING
CAKE

Wade Bradford ~ illustrated by Kevin Hawkes

CANDLEWICK PRESS

"Hello, Mr. Snore," said the bellhop. "What brings you to the Sharemore Hotel today?"

"I have been hired to play my violin at a wedding," said Mr. Snore.

"Welcome," said the wedding planner. "It's wonderful to see you."

Then she said, "You're a tad ahead of schedule. May I bring you a cup of cocoa while you wait?"

"Yes, but hold the marshmallows, please," said Mr. Snore. "They make me sneeze."

While Mr. Snore waited for his cup of cocoa without marshmallows, he noticed a dessert trolley. On it was a beautiful cake.

He also noticed a dodo bird, eyeing the icing on the cake.

The dodo hopped onto the trolley and gobbled up a frosting rose.

"Don't touch that cake!" shouted Mr. Snore, running at the bird and waving his violin bow. The dodo dashed away.

The wedding planner had seen everything. "Well done, Mr. Snore! You saved the wedding cake!"

"Oh, it was nothing," said Mr. Snore, puffing up his chest just a little bit.

The wedding planner went to find the bakers to fix the frosting.
Mr. Snore watched over the wedding cake in case the dodo returned.

The dodo did not return. But two beavers barged into the room, heading straight for the cake!

"Begone, beavers!" shouted Mr. Snore. "Don't touch that cake!"

The beavers scampered away.

Mr. Snore was feeling quite heroic until he noticed a boa constrictor slithering toward the dessert trolley.

"Stay away from that cake, you snake!"

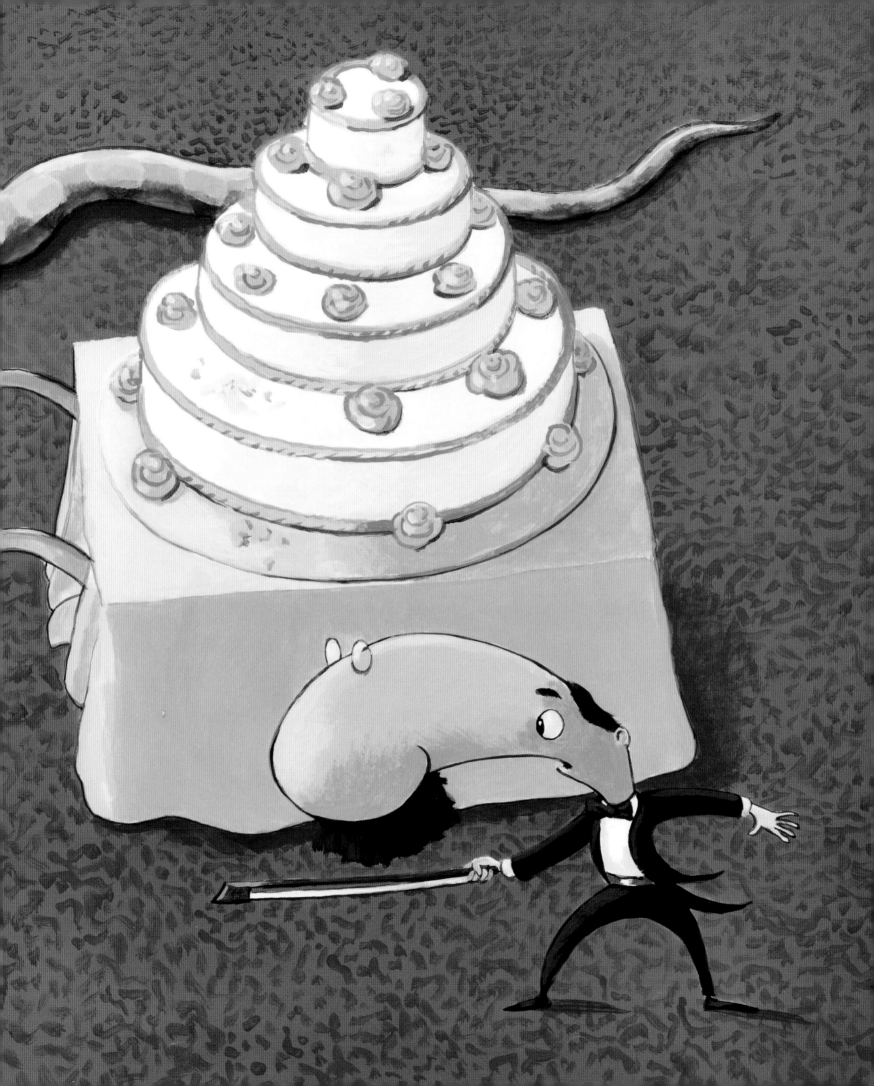

Mr. Snore fled the lobby with the wedding cake.

He ducked into what he thought was an empty room.

But it wasn't a room, and it wasn't empty at all.

To save the cake from the bats, Mr. Snore bounded out of the closet, down the hallway, and through the ballroom.

"That frosting looks delicious!" said a pelican.

"I cannot wait to have a slice!" said an ostrich.

"This cake is not for you!" declared Mr. Snore, flying past them.

Mr. Snore thought he was in the clear when, from behind him, came a mighty *Stomp! Stomp! Stomp!* Something was chasing him. Something big.

It was a dinosaur in a tuxedo. "Stop!" he boomed.
"Come back with that cake!"

Mr. Snore raced into the kitchen.

The dinosaur followed close behind and . . .

ran right into the freezer.

Mr. Snore slammed the freezer door.

The bellhop and the wedding planner heard the commotion
and rushed into the kitchen. Along with them came the bats,
the boa constrictor, the pelican, the ostrich, and the beavers.

"Look out!" Mr. Snore cried. "Those beavers will try to steal the cake."

"These beavers are the best bakers in town," said the wedding planner. "They are here to fix the frosting."

"What about the boa constrictor?" asked Mr. Snore. "What does he want?"

"He is the best man," explained the wedding planner. "And these lovely bats are the bridesmaids."

"And we are wedding guests," said the pelican and the ostrich.

THUMP!
THUMP!
THUMP!

"Then who," Mr. Snore asked with a nervous gulp, "is in the freezer?"

From behind the onlookers came a loud and thunderous wail.
"Where is my groom?"

"Oops," said Mr. Snore.

It was a beautiful wedding, with a beautiful cake,
and Mr. Snore played his violin beautifully.

So beautifully, in fact, that all was forgiven.
"You saved the cake," the bride and groom said.

They were so pleased that they gave Mr. Snore the first slice.

Unfortunately, the frosting was marshmallow.

"Gesundheit," said the dodo, who was definitely NOT on the guest list!